I Can Read *Comics* introduces children to the world of graphic novel storytelling and encourages visual literacy in emerging readers. Comics inspire reader engagement unlike any other format. They ask readers to infer and answer questions, like:

1. What do I read first? Image or text?
2. Why is this word balloon shaped this way, and that word balloon shaped that way?
3. Why is a character making that facial expression? Are they happy, angry, excited, sad?

From the comics your child reads with you to the first comic they read on their own, there are **I Can Read *Comics*** for every stage of reading:

Simple stories for shared reading.

Engaging stories for children reading on their own.

Complex stories for independent readers.

The magic of graphic novel storytelling lies between the gutters.
Unlock the magic with...

I Can Read *Comics*!

Visit **ICanRead.com** for information on enriching your child's reading experience.

I Can Read *Comics* Cartooning Basics

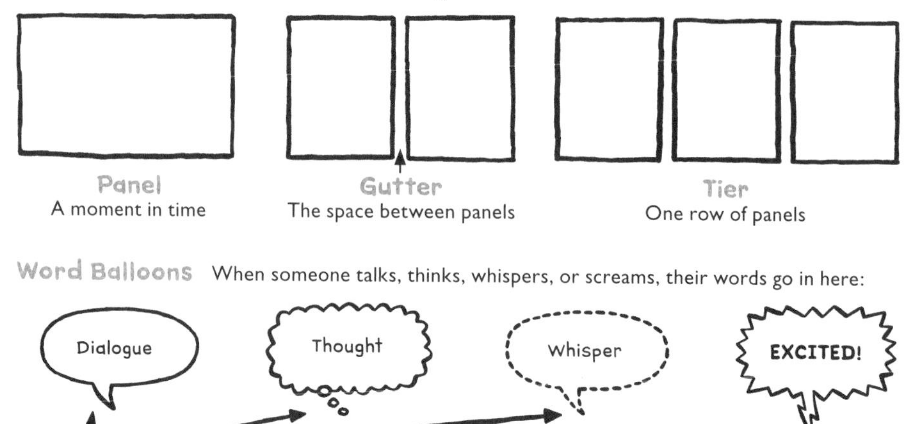

Panel
A moment in time

Gutter
The space between panels

Tier
One row of panels

Word Balloons When someone talks, thinks, whispers, or screams, their words go in here:

Tails
Point to whoever is talking / thinking / whispering / screaming / etc.

A quick how-to-read comics guide:

Remember to...

Read the text along with the image, paying close attention to the character's acting, the action, and/or the scene. Every little detail matters!

No dialogue? No problem!

If there is no dialogue within a panel, take the time to read the image. Visual cues are just as important as text, so don't forget about them!

HarperAlley is an imprint of HarperCollins Publishers.
I Can Read® and I Can Read Book® are trademarks of HarperCollins Publishers.

My Little Pony: Izzy Comes Home

For information address HarperCollins Children's Books, a division of HarperCollins Publishers, 195 Broadway, New York, NY 10007.
www.icanread.com

Library of Congress Control Number: 2021950880
ISBN 978-0-06-303751-9

Book design by Elaine Lopez-Levine
22 23 24 25 26 LSCC 10 9 8 7 6 5 4 3 2 1 ❖ First Edition

MEGAN ROTH   AGNES GARBOWSKA

An Imprint of HarperCollinsPublishers

DEAR UNICORNS AND PEGASI!
YU HAVE FRIENDS IN MARETIME BAY
COME VISIT US!
Good morning, Izzy!
Morning, Sunny!

What are you doing?
I'm listening to my music box.

It's from my home in Bridlewood. Sometimes I miss home.

I remember Bridlewood! Why don't we take a trip there today?
That's an amazing idea, Sunny!

I'm going to show you all my favorite places.
I can't **wait**!

La, la, laaa!
A road trip **always** needs good snacks.

Come on!
The Bridlewood Bakery
is just around the corner.

The friends galloped into the bakery.
Then Izzy spotted her favorite treats.
Look!
Look!

You have to try
the dazzleberry tart!

Next the friends headed to the glitter store.
Isn't glitter magical?

Let's cast a glitter spell!

CRYSTAL
TEA ROOM

And you already know the Crystal Tea Room.

I remember! Two cups of tea, please.

A little while later . . .
This is the Bridlewood School.

What was your favorite class?
Art, of course!

Finally the friends made their way back to Izzy's house.

I remember this place!
We dressed up as Unicorns here.

I'm so glad we came, Sunny.

Me too.
But . . .

I'm starting to feel worried.
Why are you worried, Sunny?

You have so many memories here.

Would you be happier here?

I **am** happy here.
But . . .
. . . I'm happy in Maretime Bay, too.

Home is where my **best friends** are.

I can't wait to get back to Maretime Bay.

Me too!
I already miss
Zipp, Pipp,
and Hitch!
Home,
here we come!